THE SECRET LETTER

JOANNE AUSTEN BROWN

Title: The Secret Letter (First Published in "Sweet Christmas Secrets Anthology 2021"—Republished as a Novella 2022)

Copyright © 2021 Joanne Austen Brown

BOOKS BY JOANNE AUSTEN BROWN

Always Louisa ~ Book One: Always Series

Always Elspeth ~ Book Two: Always Series

Rachael's Jaunt ~ Book One: Come with Me

Molly's Laird ~ Book Two: Come with Me

To all those who have loved my stories.

CHAPTER 1

"So dear brother, explain it to me again."

"We are all looking for a wife."

"Some of you are, I for one am not."

"Do not get picky, brother. The majority are and we want to find out more about the young ladies being presented. We can only do that if we all present a united front."

Thomas Wright, Viscount of Huntly, sighed. His younger brother had way too many leadership skills. He looked at some of the young men that his brother had organised to go along with his scheme. He shook his head, trying to fathom what his brother was able to do. But he had, list in hand, with the agreement of all twenty to follow the rules. Signed by each one. He could hardly say no after his younger brother, Jasper, had arranged the whole thing. He had even got his twin brother, Edmond, who usually had his head buried in a book, to go in for the crazy idea.

"Before I agree, please read out the rules again."

"Gladly. *1. You must always remain anonymous.*

2. You must not hint at your identity in your missives.

3. You must watch and listen to your young lady to see if they can guess your identity.

4. You must keep the secret of all the men.

5. You must stop writing when you have determined if the young lady is for you or not. You must keep up the pretence until all are ready to reveal themselves."

"Interesting, I must admit. And each man has chosen a potential bride from the young ladies? But what of me? I do not wish to marry. What part do you want me to play?"

"We have the perfect match for you. Miss Cora Fitzgibbon."

"You are joking. Cold Cora? It is out of the question." He shook his head.

"Why? You said yourself you want no woman for wife. She wants no man for husband. All you need to do is write the letters that she will probably ignore. But we believe she will be intrigued. Then you will need to keep her occupied so that I may have a chance of capturing her sister's heart. Lillian's." His brother sighed and he watched his eyes glaze over as he thought about the lovely Lillian.

After a moment Jasper continued, "Besides, as a renowned London rake, we thought you of all people could be the one who unfreezes Cora. And it is summer, so the weather is on your side."

"That is a challenge I believe most men would pass on…"

"But Thomas you will not, will you? You love a challenge."

Thomas looked around at the gathering of young gentlemen. Not all twenty but a large number. Each were watching and waiting for his response. He shrugged.

"Very well. Tonight, I will watch my prey and tomorrow we will all send the first letter. Agreed?"

"Agreed. Thank you, Thomas. You will not regret this."

"We shall see." He looked at all the smiling faces and shook his head.

* * *

THE UPTON BALL was a big squeeze. The first major ball of the season. For the last week small introductory balls had occurred but this one was the major event and would kick off the season. Tonight, he would watch Miss Cora Fitzgibbon. Cold Cora. He could not understand why she displayed such disdain. She was beautiful to be sure but did not allow any man to obtain a foothold around her. What was her problem?

Thomas took out his pencil and a small notebook. He jotted down some of his observances and thoughts.

. *Beautiful*

. *Cherry coloured lips, probably make up.*

. *Black raven coloured hair*

. *The deepest of blue eyes*

. *Tall and slender*

He stood nearby her to listen to her conversations. He was surprised at the numerous conversations about the weather and politics. She was more intelligent than most young ladies. She seemed very serious, and he wondered if he could make her laugh

. *Intelligent*

. *Make her smile and laugh*

Perhaps she was cold. Or perhaps she just did not want to deal with fools. He understood that kind of thinking. He rarely attended these events because he could not stand the matrons who attempted to catch him for their simpleton daughters. He was careful to avoid most of them. But he now watched the most well-known making her way straight toward him. Lady Sarah Pinkerton.

"Viscount Huntly, Lord Thomas Wright. What an honour to have you attend the ball of the season. On the prowl, are we?"

He bowed.

"Lady Pinkerton, what a pleasure to see you. No, I am here giving my brothers moral support. Their first season."

"Oh, the twins are here. Do introduce me, dear boy."

He offered the lady his arm and escorted her to where some of the young men had planted themselves.

"Lady Pinkerton. May I introduce you to my brothers, Jasper, and Edmond."

Both young men looked at him as if they had seen a giant enter the room. Then they bowed to the matron.

It was then he noticed the two young ladies standing behind her, who had followed on her coat tails, well on the hem line anyway.

"May I introduce you young gentlemen to Miss Amber Pinkerton, my niece, and Miss Lillian Fitzgibbon."

He stood back so that he could observe the meeting. His brothers bowed but showed interest only in Miss Fitzgibbon. He had no trouble in seeing that. Miss Pinkerton was somewhat weighty and kept her head bowed. She lacked confidence.

"May I have the next dance, Miss Fitzgibbon?" His brother Jasper began his pursuit.

"Yes sir, I would be pleased to."

Jasper presented his arm, and she placed her hand upon it, and they went to the dance floor. To his surprise his brother Edmond addressed Miss Pinkerton.

"Miss Pinkerton, would you do me the honour of having a dance with me?" he asked in a hushed tone.

She lifted her head, blushed, and nodded.

"I would be delighted, sir."

Edmond also offered his arm which she took, and they too made their way to the dance floor. He made a mental note to ask Edmond who he had his eyes on.

"There, two more young ladies taken care of. Please excuse me,

Viscount Huntly, but I need to get some other young ladies involved. Can I interest you in one?"

He jumped at the opportunity to be formally introduced to his prey.

"I would appreciate an introduction to Miss Cora Fitzgibbon, Lady Pinkerton."

"Oh, that will be interesting. Come with me."

They made their way back to the other side of the ballroom. He watched as Cora's face turned red as they made their way to her position. He could see that she had been observing them. Maybe she was expecting their attack now.

"Miss Cora Fitzgibbon, may I introduce you to the Viscount of Huntly, Lord Thomas Wright."

She looked at him coldly. All blushes had disappeared.

He stood at a precipice that would either devour him or he would conquer.

Was he ready? Definitely.

"Miss Fitzgibbon, my pleasure."

He bowed then, stood, and looked directly in her eyes.

To his surprise, she acknowledged him.

"My lord, the pleasure is mine."

He had not expected to be acknowledged due to his reputation. There was a spark in her eyes, but he could not determine what it was in relation to. Interest? He doubted it.

"Would you do me the honour of dancing the next waltz with me?" he asked for the waltz as it was a romantic dance. In fact, the *ton* thought it scandalous so he thought she would probably decline. Despite its scandalous reputation, each ball still had the dance played two or three times per night.

"Why..." she hesitated. Not something any young lady should do in front of a matron of the *ton*.

Lady Pinkerton did not disappoint.

"Come now, Miss Cora. You are not frightened of dancing with a well-known rake, surely?"

He watched her steely resolve take hold. Those words were fighting words and she looked ready to march into battle. This was becoming exciting.

"I will be delighted, your lordship."

She curtsied and turned and walked away. The cold shoulder had been given. He was paying attention.

"Good luck with that one, Viscount. You will need it."

Lady Pinkerton turned and sauntered away. He stood there watching Miss Cora continue her retreat to the other side of the room. She had been forced into a dance she did not want to have. But he was looking forward to it now. A chance to get up close and personal to his prey. How would she respond? This job was turning out to be far more exciting than he had anticipated.

CHAPTER 2

All Cora wanted to do was hide. The hot flush again crossed her face. The heat was intense. Why had she accepted the rogue? She was a fool. The shock of being introduced to the most well-known rake of London society and a man who she had secretly wanted to have, had shown interest in her. It had placed her on the back foot. A place she did not usually occupy.

She had put on her cold disinterested face but that was not going to put him off. He smiled and a prickling sensation travelled up and down her back. Why was he paying her attention? Her concerns were rising.

She sat on the chair in the corner. As the music finished her sister came and joined her. She was escorted by a handsome young man. He bowed to them both and departed.

"Oh Cora, I just had a dance with Jasper Wright. He was very polite and seemed delighted to dance with me. He is nothing like his rakish brother. All politeness. He has asked me to dance the waltz. Can I please?"

Cora looked at her sister, why was the rake's brother dancing with her sister? And why the waltz?

"Yes, but you will dance close to where I will be."

"Are you going to dance the waltz? With whom?"

"Do not sound so shocked, Lilly. I do dance."

"I know you do, but the waltz? So many of the *ton* hate the dance."

"Yes, the waltz."

"Are you feeling alright, Cora?" She lifted her hand and touched her sister's forehead.

"I hesitated and Lady Pinkerton threw me in with the sharks."

"Who are you dancing with?"

"Viscount Huntly."

Lilly's face looked stricken as she drew her hand to her mouth to cover her shock.

"I know and the biggest shark in the ocean took hold, and I could not get away."

"But such a compliment, dear Cora. I told you that you would attract many men."

"But he is a rake, not marriage material and besides, I do not want to marry. Nor do I wish to be pursued by a rake."

"I understand. You are here to protect me. But you could do worse. He is so very handsome. Perhaps he is here to observe and protect his brothers. So, he might not be looking for a wife. Just entertainment."

"Do not put those silly ideas in your head, sister. He is not safe. Whatever reason he is here I do not like the fact that he made a bee line toward me. I will take care of him. I plan to be no one's entertainment. You start watching the others for a possible good match for yourself."

"Yes, Cora."

Lilly could be so naïve as to the rakes and other men of the *ton*. She just adored them if they were handsome. A significant problem if the rakes got the wrong message.

She sat back and looked at the dancing forms in front of her.

Soon she would be in the arms of a well-known rake and probably be condemned by the rest of the society for agreeing to dance with him. A long sigh left her lips. A dream she had long held was about to come true. No one was looking so would not see her excitement. She needed to be careful.

* * *

THOMAS WAS WATCHING her relax in the corner with her sister. Her sister was attractive in a girlish kind of way. But too young for his liking. He wanted an equal. Someone who could hold her own and still be the perfect lady. Had he found her? This was unexpected. He was attracted to the Cold Cora. He shook his head, and a groan escaped his lips. She was not for him even though he was attracted. He did not want to marry, and this was a joke anyway. He was helping his brothers not himself.

And then the moment came. The waltz was announced. Jasper came to stand next to him.

"I will be dancing with Lillian if her sister will allow it. Please help her to allow it."

"You need not fear little brother. I will be waltzing with Miss Cora."

"How on earth did you manage that?"

"Lady Pinkerton introduced us, and she could not resist."

"Oh, brother you really are the greatest rake in London. You snagged Cold Cora."

"Do not address her with that name." He kept his voice low but menacing. "I definitely felt some warmth from her."

"Then let us take our charges and dance up a storm."

"Lets."

He straightened his gloves and walked to where he knew she was sitting.

"Miss Fitzgibbon, you promised to have this dance with me."

"Ah, yes sir."

Cora stood and he gazed into her eyes. Those deep blue eyes, like great oceans, holding promises of more than just cold water. He took her to a spot on the floor and brought her into his arms, ever so gently. Now he had her undivided attention. He could feel her gloved hand firm in his. His other hand gently placed on her back. He was almost certain he could hear her heartbeat. She smiled and the music began.

They moved slowly and the rest of the room disappeared. He continued to gaze into her eyes, and she was staring into his. This attraction between the two dominated the room. He was sure that every person in the ballroom had eyes only for the two of them. He needed to be careful. But their attraction was electric.

* * *

THE WARMTH of his gloved hand penetrated the silk of her dress. The music started and he slowly swept her away. How had she captured his attention? His dark hair shone in the candlelight. His eyes were deep green like the bed of a forest floor. She wanted to dive into his eyes and roll on the green bed.

What was she thinking?

He drew her in closer and their bodies touched. Energy zipped through her. She could not deny it. His body was enticing and warm. All too soon the music had stopped, and they continued to stare at each other. Lilly's voice finally penetrated her thoughts.

"Thank you, Cora, for allowing Jasper to give me my first waltz."

"It is my pleasure to dance with you." She heard Jasper say.

She let go of Thomas' hand. But she grabbed Lilly's. Her legs were shaking, and she was sure she would fall.

He offered her his arm and escorted her back to her seat. Lilly trailed next to her, and she assumed Jasper was not far behind.

"Thank you, Miss Fitzgibbon. I may come back and dance the

next waltz if you will allow me?" His voice flowed smooth like honey.

She smiled as she looked into his eyes.

"Most certainly."

She looked at Jasper.

"And you may dance with Lillian again if you wish?"

"Thank you, Miss Fitzgibbon. I would be delighted to."

Both men bowed and left them to their thoughts.

"Cora. You are in love with him?"

She gave herself a shake.

"Do not be so foolish, Lilly. I do not fall in love."

"Well, whatever it is, I like it. I will get to dance with Jasper again."

"Yes, you will."

She breathed out a long slow breath. One that she could imagine she had been holding on to for years. She watched his departing form and longed to be held by him again.

CHAPTER 3

$\mathcal{A}$s Cora lay wide awake in bed all she could see in the darkened room were the forest green eyes of a certain rake. Why? Because she allowed him to get too close. But the dancing they had done? Another waltz and a country dance. She had been captivated by him and he gave every indication that he was captivated by her. This did not bode well. He probably wanted to mark her as the next notch on his bed post. And that was not going to happen.

* * *

Sleep had eluded her for some hours, but she had finally dropped off. As she got dressed for the morning her sister came dashing into the room.

"Look Cora, we both have letters. I wonder who they are from? There is no indication and the butler said that no name was left. I wonder if it could be from Jasper?"

"It is probably an invitation to another ball." She placed the hair pin securely in place. "Read yours aloud."

"Very well." Lillian picked open the non-descript seal.

"*My dearest Lillian*, oh this is so exciting.

My dearest Lillian,

I watched you from afar last evening. Your beauty is obvious to all who look on you. I will be watching you, waiting for the right moment when I can reveal my love for you.

I believe that we are meant to be together.

Your secret admirer.

Cora, this is strange. Who could this be from? I only danced with Jasper and another young gentleman called Mr. Peter Collins. He showed little or no interest in me. He barely said a word."

"Lilly, it may or may not be either. You cannot respond so you will need to wait until he reveals himself."

"Please read yours?"

"As I said I am sure that it is an invitation."

"Oh, please Cora?"

"Very well." She opened the letter.

"*My Cora,*

Your beauty out shone every maid at the dance last evening. I was smitten by you. I want to spend more time with you, but you have no idea who it is that is in love with you. I will hide from you and observe, waiting for the moment that I might capture you.

Your servant,

Your secret admirer.

This is ridiculous. It must be some kind of jest. No one would send me such a letter."

"I would guarantee you anything that your letter is from Viscount Huntly. He could not get his eyes off you last evening. Let alone his hands while you danced."

"That is ridiculous. The man is a rake. He can have any woman he likes. Have you heard of any rake behaving in this manner? Writing secret love letters. And besides, I danced with him several times. That is hardly hiding from me. No, this has to be a jest or such."

"Well, we will need to keep our eyes open to whoever they are."

"I am sure that it is a jest."

But she was not sure. Who would waste their time on such a prank? Why had they both received notes from secret admirers? Her suspicions were aroused. She needed to find out what was going on.

* * *

HER SISTER LILLIAN and some of the other young ladies were having ices at Gunter's this morning and she had agreed to accompany them. Their carriage was just pulling up in front of the establishment when she noticed a group of young men walking toward them. And there in the middle, tall and straight was Viscount Huntly.

Thomas came to the door of the carriage and opened it for them.

"Lord Huntly." She acknowledged.

"Please Miss Cora, call me Thomas."

"Thomas," she said reluctantly. "This is a surprise."

"I was thinking much the same thing, Miss Cora."

"Are you and your brothers attending Gunter's?" She looked at Lillian who was blushing like a tomato, red.

Someone must have said something.

"We are but we will not disturb you."

"Oh sister, can the gentlemen not join us?"

She frowned at Lillian.

"No Miss Lillian, we will allow you some time to yourselves. Will you be attending the Sandshaw ball on Thursday evening?"

He was all politeness.

What did this rake want of them?

Her sister responded before she could intervene.

"We will, sir."

"Then may I have the pleasure of dancing the first cotillion with you, Miss Lillian?"

Lillian looked at her and smiled. She nodded her head.

"Yes, your lordship. I will be delighted."

Cora looked at Lord Huntly with suspicion. Was he writing to her sister trying to bed her? Who else could write a letter like the one they received? Well, it was not going to happen on her watch.

"Miss Cora, would you promise the first Scottish reel to me and perhaps the first Quadrille?"

She smiled and could see that he was trying to indicate his interest in her and not her sister by asking for two dances.

"I will be happy to place your name down for both, sir."

He took her hand to help her down the steps of the carriage.

She noted that he took his time to let go of said hand.

He bowed and turned to enter Gunter's, his brothers and some other gentlemen following like sheep behind him.

Lillian came to stand next to her. Essie and Daphne, Lillian's friends came to join them, as they exited their carriage that had just arrived behind theirs.

"Was that Lord Huntly?" Essie asked.

"It most certainly is," Lillian replied.

They followed the gentlemen inside.

* * *

THOMAS WATCHED them from the other side of the establishment. He had no idea the ladies would be here. Then he remembered that Jasper had suggested they meet here. Obviously, he and his Miss Lilian had been discussing many things.

"So did you all send your letters?" Each of the gentlemen nodded.

"As did I."

"I think that we will need to observe them carefully at the ball on Thursday to see what reaction they have." His brother Jasper added.

"I do not believe that we will need to wait that long. Do not turn around, I said do not turn around. I can see them clearly from here and each lady has a letter in her hand, except Cora."

"Well, what else do you see?"

"They are all a flutter. It would seem the letters were not something they expected. Cora is speaking to them; I can imagine what she must be saying."

"Well, what do you think she is saying? Don't leave us so high and dry, brother."

"She is frowning and looking this way. Do not turn your heads gentlemen, less you give us away." The young men stared at him, and all appeared devastated.

He could sense their disappointment. "We cannot hear what they are saying. I agree we need to see how they react at the next ball. Just be patient and see how they greet you."

"I do hope you are right, Thomas."

The waiter made his way to them, and he ordered ices for all, as his friends sulked, heads leaning in their hands, around the table.

* * *

"You all received a secret admirer letter? Let me have a look at them." She examined and read each one. The handwriting was different on each letter. So that ruled out one person writing the letters.

"I cannot imagine why you should all get such a letter. This is most unusual."

"And Cora received one also," her sister announced.

"Have you?" Daphne asked. "Has this ever happened before? I mean in other years?"

"Not that I am aware of. It seems like the men are combining to see what you young ladies might be thinking. After all they have not taken their eyes off us since we arrived. They are most intrigued."

"Well, what are we to do?" Essie shook her head and lowered her gaze.

"There is nothing we can do yet. None have revealed who they are nor have they made a move to reveal themselves. We will need to watch and wait. I will talk to some of the other chaperones and find out how many other young ladies have had letters."

"Do you really think this is some kind of jest?" her sister asked.

"I do not know. But it is strange. Very strange."

The waiter brought their order of ices and they all relished in its delight. She could see the gentlemen looking toward them.

What was going on?

CHAPTER 4

Thursday evening soon arrived, and Lillian and she had heard from several of the other young ladies, that they too had received a letter from an admirer. The evening was cool which was a relief as the Sandshaw ball would be well attended. So, the squash would be more bearable. If there were a great deal of people, the likelihood was she could keep a distance between them and the men who were paying them attention. She herself was convinced as to who was writing the letters.

Lillian had been on tenterhooks all day awaiting the time they could leave for the ball. The carriage ride was not long, and the lines of guests moved quickly into the ball. No sooner had they been announced than the Huntly brothers appeared near their sides.

"Miss Cora and Miss Lillian, what a delight to see you here."

His voice sounded calm and tempered. He knew they would be there and had obviously been waiting for them to appear.

"Sweet Lillian, can I get a drink for you and Miss Cora?" Jasper was looking expectantly at her.

"That would be most acceptable, Mr. Wright. We will wait for you near the balcony door," Cora remarked.

Jasper and his brother Edmond bowed then turned on their heels, heading for the refreshments.

The sultry Thomas offered his arm to her, and she placed her hand on it. Immediately a great sensation entered her body. She caught his glance and the grin. Had he sensed her reaction? What on earth was her body doing? She shook her head and did not look back at his lordship. She would not give him that pleasure.

There were some chairs near the door to the balcony to which his lordship directed them.

Thomas sat down between her and Lillian. He addressed her.

"I must say Miss Cora, that the colour gold is so very becoming on you."

"Thank you, sir."

She looked at him. He was magnificently attired in a black coat and vest of green. The vest had traces of gold woven into the design that matched the gold of her dress. She smiled seeing the connection. But she had to get to the bottom of this secret letter. And did not waste any time.

"I am delighted that you are here, sir. I was hoping, after we have partaken of the dancing you would accompany me to the balcony where we may have a private conversation."

His eyebrow lifted and his crooked smile captivated her. It was enticing in a way she had never experienced before.

"Why certainly, Cora."

Her name was spoken slowly and with delight in each syllable spoken. He was practically purring.

Jasper and Edmond appeared in front of them and offered her and Lillian a drink. Miss Pinkerton came and sat next to Lillian and Edmond handed her a drink. She smiled to see the younger men besotted by the ladies from whom they could not hide their delight and feelings for them.

They were having lively conversation and she brought up the secret letters to see if the gentlemen gave any reaction.

"Why Miss Cora, this is so fascinating. I wonder who could be behind them?"

"Do you not know, sir?"

He looked deep into her eyes.

"I am sure I do not, madam."

She saw no truth. She could see a twinkle in his eyes. He knew. Now she was determined to find out who was writing her notes.

* * *

THOMAS SMILED as he stood and took the glasses from the young ladies and gave to the waiter standing nearby. A cotillion was announced, and he offered his hand to Miss Cora. She placed her hand in his and that charge of power and attraction hit him again. He could see that she too could feel it. In all his years of raking he had never once felt that pull, that attraction that could not be explained.

She was beautiful. Pearls around her neck and woven into her hair. She also had fine golden thread that was woven into her dress, beautifully woven into her hair as well. She was stunning. He could not deny it.

"The weather has been fine since we saw you at Gunter's. I need to ask you, was Jasper told we would be attending Gunter's?"

She cut to the chase. She had gone straight to the topic she wanted to talk about, without a pause.

"I believe…it may have been mentioned."

"I do hope that there will be no more coincidences without us making arrangements?"

She twirled onto her neighbour and then twirled back.

"I do believe that the initiative was taken by Jasper. I will speak kindly to him to…"

"I would just like to know of any plans beforehand," she added. "I am not fond of surprises."

"I will make sure that you are kept informed if they have any further plans." He bowed his head.

As the music finished, he offered his arm to her.

"Can I suggest that we take our moment on the balcony. It would appear our youngers are continuing to dance."

"Yes, let us." She sounded so formal.

And suddenly he was sure that he was going into a lion's den. It was a most peculiar sensation. They went out through the doors to the balcony and over to the railing. Was this a cage she had brought him too?

"I will come to the point, sir. Why are you writing secret letters to my sister?"

He looked deep into her eyes. And frowned.

"I am not."

She shook her head. "You are. You want to make my sister one of the notches on your bedpost."

He was shocked. Cora honestly saw him as a villain. He was bewildered and a little angry.

"What makes you think it is I?"

"You are using your brothers to help you. Probably teaching them all your tricks so they too might become rakes like yourself."

"I will admit that I have been a rake as you say, but for some months now I have given up that pastime for reasons that are my own. And can you truly see my brother Edmond as a rake?"

"You expect me to believe you?" She placed her hands on her hips and had a look on her face that dared him to contradict her conclusions.

"What I expect, Cora is that you might listen to what I am saying and understand me. I have no interest in your sister."

She lowered her hands from her hip.

"If it is not you, then who is writing to my sister?"

"I thought the question might have been who is writing to you?"

Her face went as red as her lips.

"How did you…"

He realised that the gentlemen's plans might be revealed if he could not move her to another topic. He did not know what overtook his mind, but he grabbed her and kissed her fair on the mouth.

At first, she struggled but soon she was melting into his embrace. After what seemed to be ages, he pulled away from the kiss to look at her features. Her eyes were still closed. She took a breath and opened her eyes and slapped him across his face.

Cora straightened her dress and turned and walked away. He stood there watching her walk away and holding his stinging face. At that moment he knew that he loved her with all his heart.

* * *

CORA WAS ELATED. Thomas had kissed her senseless and she had allowed it. Well, at least till she had slapped him. But since then, he had been always close by and could not take his eyes off her. And when she looked back, he smiled. It was an interesting grin.

Thomas approached her as they announced the waltz. Darn. She had forgotten that she had promised him that dance. After that kiss she was not sure that she wanted to be that close to him.

Cora took his arm, offered to her, and went again to the dance floor. He was looking into her eyes as he placed his hands around her. Again, she could feel the warmth of his hand around her waist.

"I am not sorry I stole that kiss. In fact, it was wonderful."

She looked into his green eyes. Again, she saw herself rolling around in the green leaves of a forest bed, with him. She gave a little cough.

"I am not sorry I slapped you. You took a liberty that was not granted to you."

"Yes, but it should have shown you I have no interest in your sister."

"Perhaps, you plan to make a fool of me?"

"No one in their right mind would dare to make a fool of you."

"Are you being condescending?"

"No. On the contrary I am paying you a compliment. You know your mind and protect your sister. I salute you."

"You are being condescending."

He stopped dancing.

And there Thomas took her face in his hands and said again, "No, I admire you more than you can know." He placed a light kiss on her lips and continued the dance.

She glanced around at the other guests to see them both shocked and smiling. The warmth of her embarrassment rose to her face.

She was not going to slap him again as that action would only draw unwanted attention to them both. Just like his kiss had. She sighed.

He was telling the truth. She had seen that in his eyes. She pondered as they continued to dance. Who were the gentlemen that were writing to her and all the other young ladies? It would seem she had an admirer in the man who held her close and another that right now could be watching them dance.

CHAPTER 5

$\mathcal{S}$itting in front of her mirror she examined her refection while her maid continued to do her hair. He liked her, but why? Was he telling her the truth; he had given up raking, for his own reasons? All she had wanted for years now was to be one of his interests. Not to accept him but to embarrass him. Men like him thought they could have any woman they wanted. She wanted to teach him and other men a lesson. But she had weakened and was attracted to him. It was all very confusing.

Now he wanted her, did he? Even now, after having been kissed till she was senseless, she doubted his motives.

Lillian rushed into the room holding the expected letters. She handed the one addressed to her.

"You read yours first, Cora."

"No Lilly. Let me hear what your admirer has to say."

"Very well.

My dearest Lillian,

You looked so beautiful at the ball last evening. The pale lavender of your dress was so becoming. I watched you all evening. Your smile, your laughter, your attention to all who spoke to you. I am falling in love with you. I cannot tell a lie.

Your secret admirer.

Oh sister, is this beyond all hope?"

"Lillian, you cannot be falling in love with a man you do not know?"

"I am certain, sister, that Jasper is my admirer."

"What makes you so certain?"

"What man would say lavender about my dress? They would say purple or even blue. But I kept calling it lavender in front of Jasper and behold he has written lavender."

"That is an interesting theory." She pondered for a moment. "Arrange for the young ladies to meet again at Gunter's tomorrow. I have an idea."

"Ahhh Cora, I could see you thinking. I will send them notes immediately. Shall I say eleven in the morning?"

"Yes and no men had better show up. We need to find out once and for all who are writing to us. And my plan will hopefully reveal who they are. But we do not want them getting wind of the plan. Understand?"

"Yes Cora."

Lillian ran from the room.

Gingerly she opened her love note.

My Cora,

Yes, I call you, my Cora. After last evening I have no doubt that you are the woman for me. Your golden appearance captured me from the moment you arrived at the ball. I will reveal myself to you soon and I hope that the revelation will lead to a greater awareness of my feelings for you.

Yours always.

Your secret admirer.

This was disconcerting. Who was this stranger that dared to say she belonged to him? She belonged to no man. Placing the note in the drawer, she dismissed her maid and then went down to breakfast.

* * *

"GIRLS, please do not be disturbed. I have thought about this a great deal. We want them to reveal themselves, do we not?"

"Of course, we do, Cora." Her sister looked at all the young ladies, who were all nodding. "But how do we get them to reveal themselves?"

"It was you who gave me the idea, Lillian."

"Me? What did I say or do?"

"You were right to say that men do not know the specifics of the colour of our dresses. That they generalise, rather than be specific. Afterall clothing, especially of women, is hardly of an interest to them."

"Yes, but how can that help us?"

"Tomorrow night is the Bradford ball. It is a masquerade ball. I suggest that we all dress in the same colour dresses and have the same colour masks. I got these this morning. It was the one colour that they had enough masks for each of us."

She lifted a box to the table and took off the lid. Each young lady stood and investigated the box.

"Are you sure about this, Cora?"

"I am. If we stick to the plan and only call the colour plum, then yes, I think we can determine who these gentlemen are. I am convinced that the young men paying you attention now, are those gentlemen writing the letters. So, call it plum and see if they use that word in the next letter to you."

"That is ingenious. Oh, Cora you are smart."

"But we must be diligent. Correct them if they call the colour red, or burgundy, or orange. Call it plum. If you do not have a plum-coloured dress, then wear white or cream or black. But no other colour. We must concentrate on the colour of our mask. Plum."

"Yes Cora," they all said in unison.

* * *

THE BRADFORD BALL was a squeeze just as the others had been. But more exhilarating than any other ball she had attended either this year or any other year. Her body tingled as they entered the hall. For she was sure the letters were written by the gentlemen who had been paying so very close attention to them. Now they would find out for sure.

Lillian was a wash of excitement. She was sure Jasper was her secret admirer. As for herself she believed Thomas was writing her letters but did not believe for a moment, he really loved her. It felt wrong. She could not explain it. She was sure that he had other motives for doing what he was doing. And she hoped the revealing of 'plum' might tell her what he was up to.

Then she saw him. Dressed in black with a green and gold checked vest coat. His necktie was knotted to perfection. His hair was ruffled but in an attractive way. She was smitten and could not take her eyes from him. He was coming to her. She could not resist his presence. His mask only heightened his attraction. His handsome gold mask.

"Good evening Cora," he whispered and bowed to her.

"Good evening Thomas." She had finally accepted that she wanted to call him by his name.

"Ahh, but are you sure that I am Thomas?" He laughed and she laughed with him. "Shall we dance? I believe they are about to play a waltz."

He was right, again. The music played and he took her by the hand to lead her out to the floor.

Thomas drew her into his embrace, and she could feel the heat rise to her face. He always drew out a response from her. He stared into her eyes and placed his hand firmly but lovingly on her back.

"How did you know it was me. My mask is so non-descript," she asked, hoping to capture him.

"On the contrary, I would know you no matter what the colour of your mask. What colour would you call it? Fuchsia? Ruby red? Or plum."

On the word plum she looked into his eyes and at once she knew. He knew of her trap. Lillian must have told Jasper of their plan. She took her hand from his and walked off the dance floor. She turned to see if he was following her, but he stood there just staring at her.

She went out of the balcony door and over to the railing. She took a deep breath. The night was warm and the stars bright. But her disposition was ruffled. She was out of sorts. How on earth could he know her plan? To pick that colour description could not be a coincidence.

Two arms came around her. "You are playing with the wrong rake, Miss Cora."

She pulled out of the man's embrace.

"Who in heaven are you?"

He came toward her, and she placed her hands upon his chest and pushed him away.

"Now, now, Miss Cora, do not be so cold."

"Who are you?"

"Your admirer."

"You have been writing to me?"

The man shook his head. "No. What makes you say that? I just have admired you from afar. I have not been able to get close to you because Wright, the rake, will not leave you alone. His stupid game is getting in the way of all the other rakes who would love to get closer to you and some of the other young ladies."

"What game? And who the devil are you?" She pushed him away again.

"Viscount Gregory Michaels, at your service, madam." He bowed and moved in, to place his arms around her again, trapping her between him and the railing. "It is I; you should be playing with and not the Viscount Wright. Why do you allow him near you?"

She pushed him away again. "He had approached me and had himself introduced, by a member of the *ton* instead of sneaking around. If he has not left my side, I have not been complaining, but you sir…"

"And I have no intention of leaving her side again. I suggest Mr Michaels that you find your game elsewhere." Thomas stood behind the interloper.

Cora was glad to see him but annoyed that he believed he had the right to rescue her. He came and stood behind her.

"Thank you, Viscount, but I can fight my own battles. I suggest Mr Michaels as we have not been introduced and that I have no intention of being introduced to you, you leave."

She watched him smile at her then look at Thomas, frown and turn and walk away. She knew the man only departed due to some unseen threat Thomas displayed.

"Well, I thought for a moment that I had met my secret admirer."

"Who, Michaels? I would be surprised if the ape knew how to spell let alone write."

"They are harsh words? Do you find it outlandish that any man might find interest in me?"

"That madam is not what I meant, and you know it."

"Do I, Thomas?"

"We are attracted to each other and that is for certain."

"I will agree that we seem to have only eyes for each other at the moment."

He stepped closer to her.

"But that does not give you the right to stand over any other man who might show me interest."

"Would you like for me to call Michaels back?"

Thomas was standing directly in front of her now. She placed a hand on his chest.

"I do not think that is necessary, do you?"

He placed his hands around her waist and drew her closer to him.

"No. We do not need the likes of Michaels anywhere near us." And he leaned into her and kissed her.

She was floating above the world as he deepened the kiss. She had never desired any man this way before. She wanted to be with him in all senses of the word.

"Oh Cora, I want you. I need you."

"Just admit that you are my secret admirer."

"I cannot."

He was placing kisses on her neck. She was so hot she might explode any moment.

"Why?"

"I cannot tell you. I promised."

"Promised who?"

"Jasper and the other gentlemen?"

She put her hands on his chest and gently pushed him from her.

"What on earth do they have to do with what we feel for each other?" She was genuinely confused at his words.

He was looking deep into her eyes. She watched and waited.

"I will need to see if they are ready."

"Ready? Ready for what."

"I will tell you all when it is over."

"When what is over? Is this some kind of game?"

"My darling…"

"My darling nothing. What is this about?"

At that moment, her sister and Jasper came out on the balcony.

"Brother. I have spoken to all the gentlemen. We are ready to reveal. Well, I have already revealed all to Lillian. So, you can stop wooing Miss Cora."

Thomas swung around and jumped at Jasper. He grabbed him around his necktie.

"I have been keeping quiet despite everything. I want Cora and you are telling me it's over."

Cora backed away and headed toward the ballroom.

"Cora, let me explain."

She stopped and turned to face him. "There is nothing to explain. I see it all. Someone had to keep Cold Cora busy while the gentlemen were busy making love to the young ladies. I was in the way."

"No. Well yes, but that is not what happened."

"Good night, Mr Wright."

She took the hand of Lillian and walked into the ball room. Lillian was struggling and pulled her hand from her grasp.

"I will go home with Essie. I have no plans to leave."

"Fine. I will ensure that happens. I will see Essie's mother and then I will leave."

"Cora?"

"What is it, Mr Wright?" She could hear her voice getting louder.

"Please talk to me?"

"We have nothing to say, sir."

She turned and went to speak with Essie's mother and then left as quickly as she could…

CHAPTER 6

The carriage ride home was dreadful. All Cora could do was cry. And they were bitter tears. For years she had been aloof, cut off from the rest of the *ton*. She had been part of events but separate from them. And why? Because years ago, she had overheard a group of men, all well-known rakes, call her cold. From that day she was determined to be as cold as she could to any man who came near her. And she had. But in her heart, she had longed for love but was afraid to open to any man. Until Thomas Wright. Now, he had humiliated her. She was a fool and felt it through every inch of her body. She ached all over. It was all a game. How could he?

The carriage pulled up in front of her home. She dismissed all around her and went to her room. She refused all advances of her parents to tell them anything of the night. All she would impart was that Lillian was being chaperoned by Essie's mother, and would return home later.

* * *

THE NIGHT WAS dark and added to her depressing mood. The darkness was like a weight around her and pressed her down. She could not sleep, and the tears had long stopped. She was sure she had emptied the tank where tears were stored.

There was a tap at the door. It opened and a figure came toward her. She knew it was Lillian.

"Finally, home?"

"Oh, Cora. It has been a night of joy and misery."

"What on earth do you mean?"

"Jasper has asked me to be his betrothed."

"Good luck and joy to you. Now leave me alone."

"But Cora, Thomas loves you."

"No, he does not. He was there to keep me out of the way so Jasper could get to know you."

"At first that might be right, but he wants to be with you."

"Ah, the perfect words of a rake. Be with me. Not marry me. No talk of love. Lillian, can you not see the truth? He wants me as a notch on his bed. Love? The man does not know the meaning of the word. Please go to your bed and leave me."

"I will. But you are wrong."

Lillian slowly left the room.

* * *

CORA ENTERED THE BREAKFAST ROOM. It was later than usual as she had trouble sleeping. She thought that her parents and sister would have gone ahead with the rest of their day. But no. They sat at the table drinking tea and chatting in hushed voices. The conversation ceased as she closed the door.

She sat down and a cup of tea was placed in front of her by the butler. A maid brought her a small selection of items she would usually have to break her fast.

"Good morning, Cora," her father said without hesitation.

33

"Good morning father, mother, Lillian." Nodding at each of them.

She lifted her cup and took a sip of tea. The warmth reached into her cold soul and strengthened her. Closing her eyes, she allowed the warmth to flow through her body.

"Can you tell us now," her father continued, "What happened to you last evening?"

"I would rather not." She kept her eyes closed.

"Do you need more time?" asked her mother.

"I do not think there will ever be enough time."

"Well, I need to ask questions and I would appreciate some answers. Especially of Jasper Wright," her father blurted out.

"Jasper?" Her eyes opened.

"Yes, he and his elder brother are arriving shortly, I believe to ask for Lillian's hand?"

"And which gentleman wants Lillian's hand?"

"Oh, Cora dear, you know that Jasper and I have only eyes for each other."

"Then I wish you well. He is a fine young man, of good fortune and has good taste in choosing you."

"So, you recommend him to your sister?" her mother asked.

"Yes, mama. He is a good man for Lillian. I believe that his interest in you, sister, is true."

"But what of the Viscount?"

"What of him?"

"I understand that he wishes to speak with you."

"I have no interest in speaking with him." She stood and instructed the butler to serve her breakfast in the garden. And she left without another word.

* * *

THOMAS STOOD at her door with Jasper. Would Cora see him? He had his doubts. Her strong will made him sure he would be rejected. The door opened and they were ushered into the library where Lillian and her parents were waiting.

"What a delight to meet you Viscount Wright." Mr Fitzgibbon held out his hand.

He took and gave his hand a firm shake. It was not the usual greeting, but he appreciated it.

He bowed at Lillian and her mother.

"It would seem Miss Cora has no desire to meet with me?"

"I..." He watched as Mr Fitzgibbon's face grew red. The poor man was embarrassed.

"Please sir, excuse my bluntness but I am well aware of Cora's pride and stubbornness. But I will make my opinion clear. I wish to marry her. I love her. I just now have to convince her of my sincerity."

"Well sir, I thank you for your bluntness and I believe in your sincerity even if she is too blind to see it. I for one would be delighted if you can win the heart of my eldest daughter. I wish you well. Now please sit down and we will have tea."

"Thank you, sir, I will." He immediately understood he had the full support of Cora's family, to woo her. He just had to work out how. Could he ever have Cora in his arms again?

* * *

THE AFTERNOON WAS SO BEAUTIFULLY warm. Cora was thankful to be outside on such a pleasant day. The maid had brought her tea and she enjoyed the cup, despite knowing that Thomas and his brother were in the house. She would stay here and do all she could to not think about him. It was difficult as she had seen both her sister and Thomas come to the window to see her sitting in isolation. She would dearly have loved to know what they were talking

35

about. She pushed down the thought. It would do her no good to ponder.

She finished her cup and walked around the garden and forced herself to stay away from the house. She looked at the trees and the flowers and enjoyed the gentle sounds of nature and the distant sounds of horses clomping on the pebbled roads.

Then he was there walking toward her. She did not want to speak with him and returned to her seat. At least while she sat, she had the strength to deny him and ignore him. She was terrified her legs would not hold her up if she remained standing.

He bowed to her. "Miss Cora. I was wondering if you would allow me to speak with you?"

"Sir. I have no desire to speak with you. You have humiliated me once. You will not do it again."

"Cora?"

"Sir?"

"I will not give up. And please do me a favour and get off your high horse."

He turned and walked back toward the house. She sat straight and watched him walk away. Speaking to her like that was not going to make her soften her stance. Who did he think he was? She closed her mouth and tried to change the expression of shock she knew was on her face.

* * *

THOMAS CAME BACK into the library.

"She is bewildered. Quite confused. Well done, my boy." Mr. Fitzgibbon gave him a slap on the back.

"I must admit all I wanted to do was grab her and kiss her until she melted in my arms, but I agree she needs to know I will not stop pursuing her." He watched the poor man's face redden.

"I love her, sir. I am sorry if I shock you."

Thomas walked to the window and could see the confusion and anger on her face as he looked out. "I hope that I am doing the right thing."

Lillian came to stand beside him.

"Dear Thomas, she will wake to your efforts. Give her time. I will do what I can to explain so that she might stop and listen to you the next time you see her."

"I hope so, Lillian."

"Call me Lilly, after all we are almost family."

"Very well, Lilly."

It was true she would marry her brother Jasper. And he was delighted. But he now wanted to win the heart of the woman he loved.

CHAPTER 7

Thomas had called on her every day for the last week and she had refused to see him. Her temper was frayed, and she was snapping at all who came near her. Most of her time was spent in her room. But this morning she had decided she would go with Lillian for a ride in Hyde Park.

As she waited for Lillian at the stable, she again went through the events of the ball that had caused her stress. But all she could picture was Thomas' green eyes. She rested her head on the neck of her horse and closed her eyes.

"Would it be better to see his eyes in person?" Lillian whispered.

"What makes you think I see his eyes?"

"I know you and that's what you were thinking. You get a certain expression on your face when you think about his eyes. I have seen it before."

"You think you are so worldly now that you are betrothed."

"Cora, that was not a nice thing to say."

"You are right, Lillian. I am sorry."

"But I am right. You were thinking about his eyes."

"Yes, I was. Shall we ride?"

"Of course. But I wish to continue our discussion. So do not change the topic."

She laughed as the stable boys helped them to mount.

* * *

CORA CLOSED her eyes and took a deep breath. Having been indoors for all this time had settled her. She wished now that she had allowed Thomas time to tell her the truth, well the truth as he saw it. She knew the truth. She herself was not convinced of his love. Though he had come to see her every day since she had rejected him.

"I believe I should enlighten you as to the so-called game the gentlemen were playing."

"Lillian my dear, I understand what they were doing. Please do not help them to humiliate me more."

"But I do not believe that you know the whole story."

"Answer me this, did they, Jasper and the other young men, want me out of the way?"

"Yes, but not…"

"Then there is nothing more to say."

"Cora dear, I know that you have a mind of your own. In fact, I respect you for it."

"Thank you."

"It is not a compliment."

Cora pulled up her horse and just stared at her sister.

"What on earth do you mean?"

Lillian turned her horse around and rode back to her.

"I thought that you of all people would want to know the truth and not rely on assumptions and lack of facts."

"I know that I was being kept away from you so that Jasper could get close to you. Is that a fact?"

Her sister nodded.

"Then I have every right to feel cheated, humiliated and toyed with."

"But you do not know the whole truth and that clouds your judgement."

"You keep saying that. Then tell me the truth."

"He fell in love with you. Despite all reason to push you aside as but a game to be played, he loves you."

"A rake does not know love."

"On the contrary I think they know more about love than we women give them credit."

"I think, Lilly, that you are too romantic for your own good."

"Thank you. I will accept that as a compliment."

"I did not mean it to be."

"Oh, sister I know. But it is romantic and soon you will realise that there is more romance in your sphere of influence than you give yourself credit for."

"I will think on that, but I have many doubts."

They rode on.

* * *

WHEN THEY GOT BACK from their ride a note was waiting for Cora. She recognised it as the handwriting of her secret admirer, Thomas. She went upstairs to her room and placed the letter on her desk. She did not want to open it.

Picking up the book she was reading, she sat in the chair by the window. For the next hour Cora tried to distract herself. But it was to no avail. She kept reading over the same lines and thinking of green eyes. Finally, she placed the book down and went to her desk to pick up the letter. She returned to the seat and opened it.

My dearest Cora

He had a nerve.

I call you that because I love you. I know that you think me false and with my reputation I can understand why you would think that way. But today I must travel back to my family estate on business. I did not want to go, because you would see me as running away from you.

That is why I dropped this letter at your home. Every day you will receive a letter from me until I can return to London. I then hope you will allow me to see you in person.

I will try to explain my feelings and why I am so much in love with you, in these notes. Then when I return if you still do not wish to see me, I will leave you be. But my hope is that you will see my true love and respect for you.

Always

Your secret admirer.

"I do not think so Thomas Wright."

She folded the letter and went to her desk and placed it securely in the drawer. But she did want him to prove it. Her stubborn streak was beginning to fade.

CHAPTER 8

Thomas Wright, Viscount of Huntly, was true to his word. He wrote to her every day. Cora longed for the letters to arrive. She did not let anyone know how much she waited for them. There was so much excitement as the household prepared for the wedding of Lillian and Jasper. She certainly did not want to distract anyone from that excitement. But she was warming to this rake.

Dear Cora

I understand from Jasper the wedding will be held at your family estate in Oxfordshire.

It is a day that I await with great joy. Knowing how much my brother loves your sister gives me joy. I know they are both young but the love they share is clear to all who behold them. Would you not agree?

Cora did agree. She had been with Lillian everywhere as they prepared the items they needed for the wedding. Her dress, decorations for the hall. The wedding would be near Christmas so the weather would be cold. Lillian was so happy. In a matter of a few months, she had watched her young sister turn from a giggling girl to a beautiful and distinguished woman.

She knew that Thomas was still at his family estate and had been for some months. He had kept his promise. She had received a letter from him every day. But soon she and her family would be leaving the summer season behind them and returning to the country. Up until now she had not replied to any of his letters, but she wanted him to know when they were returning to Oxfordshire. She prepared a reply and hoped he would appreciate it.

Dear Thomas

Firstly, can I say that I have enjoyed receiving your letters though at first, I found them to be annoying. Surprisingly, discussing the day-to-day experiences on your estate have been a highlight. The events sound so very familiar when we are at home and not in the bustle of London. And I thought you might want to know that we will be returning to Oxfordshire Thursday week.

Your friend

Cora

* * *

"WELL BROTHER, she is warming to you." Jasper handed back the letter, he had already read for the tenth time.

"Do you really think so? I do not want to be just her friend."

"Lillian confirms that she awaits your letters daily with bated breath. She wants to hear what you have to say. That is more than she wanted before you left London."

"Then perhaps it is time that I lay my heart out completely. What do you think?"

"Thomas, you are the great lover. Why are you asking me?" Jasper laughed and walked away.

Thomas was glad that his brother was home from London. If only for a short time. He was heading back to London to escort Lillian to her home and to see where the wedding was to be held.

Thomas stood there looking at the first and only letter he had received from Cora. He placed it in his coat pocket near his heart. He let his hand rest on his heart as he made his way to the library. He had a letter to write.

* * *

SMALL NOTES ARRIVED at the London house every day until they left for Oxfordshire. Cora was glad they arrived but had noted that they were shorter and less informative than they had been up until this time. She longed to see him, to know that his interest in her had not waned. But when they had arrived at the manor house late on the afternoon, they had left London, a long and bulky letter from Thomas was awaiting her. She placed it in her room and after the rest of the family had gone to bed, she went up to read what he had to say.

Dearest beloved Cora

His address sounded so right, and she did want to tell him that. She was excited that the address sounded so right.

I wanted to tell you for some time how I fell in love with you. I ask that you read this letter in its entirety and let me know in one word how you feel. But more about that later.

Jasper had eyes on Lillian from the moment he saw her. I believe that was well before the first big ball of the season. For him it was love at first sight. As for me I wished him well. But Jasper has the ability, to organise events to go his way. He is a great leader, and I must admit I fell in with his grand design to capture your sister's heart.

He spoke so highly of a younger brother.

He had spoken to other young gentlemen about an idea they could put into action to see if the young ladies they were interested in were truly interested in them. My brother, the born leader. And you know by now the secret letters were the way to the young ladies' hearts. But he was concerned that you, my dearest would prevent them from getting close.

She began to cry. Was she really so cold hearted? She dried her tears and continued.

He approached me to agree to distract you. I agreed but made it clear that it was to distract you only. I did not want a wife.

The tears fell again in a storm of emotion that she had not expected. He did it for his brother. He did not love her. After a few moments she began to read again.

That was until the Upton ball where I watched you from afar. It was the first time I had seen you. When Lady Pinkerton introduced us, I was delighted. Not because I could get close to you as a victim of my brothers' schemes but as a woman who matched me in all that I could see. I was already attracted to you. Everything you exuded told me that you were a strong and independent person. And I admired that.

My raking days were over and still are. My father had encouraged me to marry. But I had seen no woman whom I could respect and see as equal. That was what I wanted. Not a girlish wife but a woman who could stand up to me and keep me on the straight and narrow. Then I met you and all I wanted to do was be with you. I wanted you. Not to keep me on the straight and narrow as I first thought, but to love me with all of her being. Not to be afraid but to see a life with me as an adventure we could go on together.

I was ashamed of myself that I had agreed to distract you on behalf of my brother. I did not care about the distraction, I just wanted you. As the days went on, I watched you care for your sister and the other girls. I had not deceived you. Well, not intentionally as had been planned. You are intelligent. You knew exactly what my brother was doing. You, sweet Cora, had worked it out. But I had given my word not to say a thing to you. It broke my heart. I wish I had not given my word, but I had. Then all was revealed, and you thought me a villain.

And perhaps I am. But my love for you has not abated. Dearest, Cora. My beautiful lady. It is you whom I care for. If I could change the way things had occurred, I would. I should have told you from the beginning of the plan. Forgive me.

So now, you know all. I ask you to send me a note and answer one question.

Do I stand a chance in one day marrying you? Yes or no.

You will never know how much I long for the reply. I hope and pray for the affirmative.

My Love always

Thomas

Cora closed the letter and held it close to her heart. She loved him and he still loved her. Yes, a hundred times yes.

She went and sat at her desk and pulled out a sheet of paper to reply.

She pulled the bell pull, to summon the butler.

Moments later he arrived.

"Please have this note sent to Viscount Wright immediately."

"But madam, it is very late."

"I do not care. I need to get this note to him immediately."

"Yes, ma'am."

* * *

THOMAS HAD NOT SLEPT MUCH. His note would have found her yesterday and he was curious as to her reply. Well, he was more than that, he was anxious. He had never chased a woman as much as he had pursued Cora. He did not want to be rejected. The thought of life without her in his arms did not sit well.

He heard the horse in the distance as it came galloping up the drive. He was up and at the window. It was a messenger. He waited but could not keep still, pacing back and forth in front of the window.

After a few moments there was a knock at his door.

"Come."

The butler opened the door and he could see the missive in his hand.

Jasper and Edmond came into the room behind the butler.

"What is it?" Jasper asked.

"A note from Cora." He held the missive in his hand and just looked at it as the butler left the room.

Edmund came to stand by his brother. He placed his hand on his back.

"We want what you want. Open it, we are here, regardless of the answer."

He looked at his quiet unassuming brother.

"Thank you, Edmond."

He opened the note to see the one word he hoped to see. And there written large across the page was the word. *YES*. He turned the letter around and showed it to his brothers. They began to slap him on his back.

"Good for you, Thomas."

"This is wonderful news."

CHAPTER 9

$\mathcal{I}$n the morning Thomas did not waste any time. He prepared and packed a few things and took his horse and rode to Oxfordshire. It was but a short ride, only four hours. He had a trunk sent that would arrive later.

He rode in the gate of the estate. Would he be received with a warm welcome? As he got down from his mount, Lord Fitzgibbon descended the stairs to greet him.

"My lord, I am delighted you have come. We have much to talk about."

"I am pleased to be here, sir. May I see Cora before we sit down to make any plans?"

"Of course, my boy. She awaits you in the library."

He entered the house with Lord Fitzgibbon and followed him to the library. The whole family were sitting there reading. As he entered, Lady Fitzgibbon and Lillian came to welcome him and promptly left the room dragging Lord Fitzgibbon with them.

"You came?" She stood up.

"Did you doubt it?"

"It felt like a dream. So yes, I did."

He made his way to her and took her into his arms.

"Does this feel real enough?"

"Magically real."

He bent down and kissed her. He had longed for the taste of this kiss. The memory of the last only amplified the longing for this one.

They kissed and held each other for some time. Finally, he bent down to one knee.

"My darling Cora, will you marry me?"

She went on her knees in front of him and there on their knees together she kissed him.

After a moment she looked at him and said, "Yes."

* * *

FOR MANY HOURS they walked and talked. They walked in the garden and through the woods around the house. Cora shared her dreams and interests, as did he. They spoke of where they would live and when they would marry.

"I do not want to tread on Jasper and Lillian's day. I want them to have joy." Cora looked at him, sitting beside her on the bench.

Thomas looked out over the park in front of the house. "Will you allow me to be secretive again?"

"What do you mean?"

"My dearest, I want to give us a day that we will enjoy forever. I have an idea but would ask that you allow me the opportunity to surprise you."

"Thomas dear, this is what I have dreamed of, to be with you. It took me so long to see the love you had for me. So, yes please surprise me. All I want is to be married to you."

"That sounds so wonderful. Now let us go inside and I will seek your father's permission and plan my surprise."

They made their way to the house. Thomas held her hand and

the warmth of his touch was exhilarating. Could she be this happy? Of course.

✱ ✱ ✱

THOMAS SPENT a great deal of time with Cora's father, but he had it planned.

"Are you happy with your plans?" Cora asked as he exited the library.

"Yes, my dear. Your father says it is most romantic."

She laughed. "My father? Romance was not something I have known of him. Thank you for encouraging him in that area."

"I will stay for the coming week, and have our banns read at church this Sunday. Are you happy for that to take place?"

"Of course."

"Your parents will help you with all the arrangements for our wedding. But they will not reveal the time or place. That my love is what I will do. And when I do it will be a revelation of a wonderful secret."

"I have been speaking with Lillian and she has agreed that their wedding will be on Christmas Eve. I do not want to interfere with their plans."

He took her into his arms. "Please rest easy, my love. Their joy will be for their day. I promise."

✱ ✱ ✱

THE EVENTS of the weeks leading to Jasper and Lillian's wedding were hectic. The great hall was scrubbed and polished. The décor arranged in beautiful pastel colours. Lillian and she loved the gentle colours that soon occupied the hall. The house too was prepared for family and friends.

A family gathering was planned for Christmas day, after

Lillian's wedding to allow for all the visitors to enjoy the season among friends and family.

"Are you happy, Lilly?" Cora asked.

"Oh, my dear sister. I am so happy. And for you as well. You will marry Thomas and I could not be more delighted."

"Yes. Who would have thought? We will be both sisters and sisters-in-law."

"Are you happy that you will be my maiden of honour with Thomas as Jasper's best man?"

"Of course. It gives me great delight to stand up with you."

"You do not mind that I, your younger sister will marry before you?"

"No. It took me so long to realise that I loved Thomas. Whereas you knew your heart immediately."

"But that does not change that I am the younger."

"No, but it does tell me that you perhaps were the smartest of us."

Her sister took her into her arms.

"No, we both are smart. We love the men we love."

CHAPTER 10

The sun rose on a clear sky. The morning was crisp and cold. But Lillian's wedding day had arrived. All her items for her own wedding were ready also, but that was still a very much awaited surprise. Jasper and Thomas and all their family had arrived three days ago. There had been great dinners and gatherings. But very little time for Thomas and her to talk alone.

Today that would change. Thomas would be by her side for the whole day as she sent her sister into matrimony. Then she could dream only of her own union to the man she loved.

Cora and Lillian had breakfast together in Lillian's room.

"Are you happy, Lilly?"

"I am, Cora. Very happy."

"Do you know where you will go after the wedding?"

"No." She laughed. "It seems that Jasper has taken a leaf out of Thomas' secrets book. It is all a surprise."

She laughed.

"Only a year ago I swore that I would never marry. But Thomas has changed me."

"No, not changed you. Completed you. You are still Cora."

"But now we will both be complete. Let us get ready."

* * *

THE WALK from the house to the chapel was a small one. They had planned to walk but the snow overnight had turned the park into a winter wonderland. So, the carriage would take them on the short trip to keep their slippers and clothing free of the damp snow.

As they descended from the carriage many of the villagers had gathered outside the chapel to see the sisters. It reminded her that many of their family and friends were gathered to see Lilly wed and she wished for the same for her own wedding.

"Now Lillian, Jasper awaits you at the altar of the church. Let us not keep him waiting."

* * *

WHAT A GLORIOUS DAY. After the service all had returned to the house and had eaten and enjoyed each other's company. Lillian and Jasper had just left for their secret rendezvous as a married couple. She sat beside Thomas. When would they have their day?

"I find it hard to believe that my brother Jasper is now a married man."

"And my sister a married woman. But I am delighted it is so. I wish them joy."

"And what of our joy? Do you long for us to be together?"

"You know I want that more than anything else."

"Well, my dear, it is close at hand."

"Truly?"

"Yes, all will be revealed." He reached into his coat pocket. He pulled out a missive, sealed. "In here all will come true. In here I have laid out my plan. But you must promise not to open it until the morning. Yes, Christmas morning. This is my gift to you."

She took the letter and held it next to her heart. "Then my dear, I will say goodnight. For I must sleep so that I can awaken to the surprise you have prepared for me."

Thomas stood and took her hand. Placing it on his arm he escorted her to her parents to say goodnight. Then took her to the bottom of the stairs.

"Sleep soundly my love. Surprises will awake you in the morning. Now place the letter close to your heart for that is where I will be."

"Goodnight, Thomas."

"Goodnight, dear Cora."

* * *

SHE CLOSED the door to her bedroom. And placed the letter on her bed. She changed and got ready for bed. Her mind was racing. The day that had been. What had her wonderful Thomas prepared for Christmas day? She got into bed and held the missive in her hand. Tomorrow, would all her dreams come true?

* * *

SHE WAS IN THE CHURCH, but it was dark and cold. This is not what she had expected. Thomas had promised her a surprise. But he was nowhere to be seen. She kept walking up the aisle. Still, no one to be seen. Then she saw a figure at the front near the altar. She quickened her pace. When she reached the figure, he turned around and it was Michaels...she screamed.

She was sitting bolt upright in bed. Her mother came into her room with a candle.

"My dear Cora. Are you alright?"

"Yes mama. I had a bad dream. I do not know why. But it has passed."

"Cora?" It was Thomas. He too must have heard her scream and come to see what had happened.

"Just a bad dream, Thomas."

"Lady Fitzgibbon, I mean mother. May I have a few words with Cora?"

"Of course, Thomas. I will stand at the door and keep any other who may have woken at bay. Then you will both need your sleep."

She went out the door and closed it.

"Tell me, dear. Why did you scream?"

"It is so very silly. I am not the kind of person to be frightened."

"I know that. So, what frightened you?"

"It was so strange and is fading now."

"Please my dear, tell me."

"I was walking down the aisle of the church and it was dark and cold. No one was there. Then I saw a figure near the altar and I thought it was you but when I got there it was Michaels and I screamed. That is all. Silly childish thoughts."

He sat on the bed and held her in his arms.

"I do not know why you dreamed what you did. But I believe it is time for you to read your surprise letter and then I believe you will sleep soundly."

"I can wait till the morning."

"I know but I would feel better if you would read it now. Let it be my secret revealed."

"Very well." She reached over and took the letter into her hand.

"Are you sure?"

"Yes, my dearest, I am. Read it aloud."

She opened the seal.

"My Darling Cora,

I have waited for this day. I want your surprise to give you joy and peace and most of all love.

Today, Christmas day we are to wed. What a wonderful way for you and I, to be together. To be with all our family and friends. To celebrate our love.

I will see you at the church at 10am and then you and I will be man and wife. I want you to know that for me my joy will be complete. I have many wonders to share with you, so that the day will be wonderful for you.

I remember the words of Michaels. He dared to call you Cold Cora. He does not know you. To know you is to know the warm, loving gracious Cora. My Cora. My Joy.

I love you.

Your Thomas.

She cried silent tears. He knew her innermost thoughts. She did not want to be Cold Cora. And this confirmed that she was not. He loved her.

"I want you, my dear. You are not cold. Far from it. I will meet you at the church." He stood up, leaned down, and kissed her gently on the lips.

"I know the passion, warmth and love that lies beneath the surface."

He left the room, and she could hear him gently persuading her mother to rest easy. She laid down and in no time had fallen asleep.

CHAPTER 11

Christmas day. He had chosen Christmas day to wed her. She had her breakfast in her room with her mother. Then around nine o'clock her sister, Lillian arrived.

"You knew that I would wed today?"

"We did. We travelled to the next village and stayed at the coach inn so that we could get back here in time for your big day."

"Dear Thomas. He has surprised me. I am so happy that you have not missed this day and we can be together for Christmas."

"There is so much more he has in store. Now let us get you ready."

Cora's dress had a fur lined cape to accompany it and it was so beautiful to have the fur on her skin. The fur was warm, and so snuggly. She pulled it closer, and it caressed her cheeks. A long, contented sigh left her lips.

Cora and Lilly went to the chapel in a carriage as there was still much snow. Just as they had yesterday. She saw the same smiles and joy on the faces of their friends and family. It seemed all knew and were excited to have the two weddings side by side. Another day of joy to be shared.

57

There, Thomas stood at the altar, tall and in a dark blue suit. His vest was silver. He glowed. And he was smiling the biggest smile she had ever seen him have. He was handsome and was about to become hers. The day she had longed for had come and joy abounded.

Flowers filled the chapel as they had yesterday, but they were her favourites. Yesterday had been lilies for Lilly. Today roses for Cora. Every hot house in England must have been sought, to fill the chapel with such beauty.

When they returned to the manor, the hall was clean and decorated. The servants must have worked so hard to get it ready. The same colours festooned the decorations as they had yesterday. The only difference was the many silver bows that were on or about everything in the house. Everything seemed like little packages. Christmas packages.

Lunch was a typical Christmas feast with all the frills and decoration.

As everyone sat and ate, Thomas rose to his feet.

"I want to thank you all for staying on to celebrate our wedding. And for keeping it a secret. But now I want Cora to open my special gift to her."

One of the servants came in with silver service and on the plate was a box. A silver box with a bow. She took it and unwrapped the gift. As she opened the box, bright diamonds shone up to her. It was a necklace and matching earrings. And they were in the shape of a bow.

Thomas leaned down and whispered into her ear.

"You are my gift this Christmas."

"We are each other's."

"And all because you received a secret letter."

"The best letter I have ever had."

ABOUT THE AUTHOR

Joanne loves to write and she loves to travel. She is married to Andrew and lives in Central New South Wales Australia with him and their two cats Arthur and Oscar. (Meet them on Joanne's webpage) She has two grown sons and four beautiful granddaughters. Her imagination loves to take her on various trips but mainly in the area of the regency romance.

She also loves meeting new people so do drop a line to her on:

Website Facebook Instagram Twitter

I have loved using folk law and traditional history in this series. It has spurred my imagination. I love the way the fae have developed in the story and that they too are not perfect and can give a few bad apples to history.

Having mixed marriages was an idea which was there from the beginning but the fae blood would only appear in the females. That too was my idea and I loved playing with it. If you have loved this story, then you will definitely not want to miss the final in the series "Glenna's Future". And please tell your friends about this series.

Keep a look out for it. It will appear later this year.

And just to tempt you here is the cover…

Go to my website and subscribe to my newsletter. It is only monthly so you won't be bombarded by emails.

https://www.joanneaustenbrown.com/

or join me on my Facebook page.

https://www.facebook.com/joanne.boog/

Always Louisa (Always Series Book 1)

Louisa Stapleton has been disgraced and banished from Society. She wants to return to defend herself and seize the life she desires. Her father has obtained the help of the one man she sees as her nemesis. Arriving at the house party, she has her doubts about her success in returning.

Chalanor Farraday, the Viscount Lightford, had a hand in her downfall but he was not a willing participant. To redeem his honour he wants to help her back into the society that rejected her. But she hates him. That is the last thing he wants. Can he convince her to trust him?

Can they overcome the trials that they will face so that Louisa can obtain more than she had hoped for? Neither see the figures lurking in the shadows. They want to prevent her return to society. And they have their reasons for wanting her dead. Will they succeed?

Always Elspeth (Always Series Book 2)

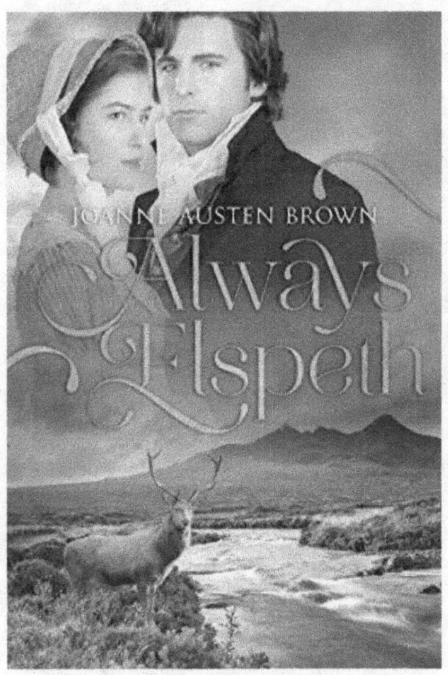

Tragedy has followed Elspeth. Hoping for a new life she moves to the Isle of Skye. Can the society that she hates leave her to start again? What she cannot see is someone who is following her.

James has loved her all his life. Elspeth rejected him once but now she may be tempted to try love again. But in the shadows, someone is stalking her.

Can James and Elspeth renew the love they once had? And make it stronger? Or will the darkness overtake them?

stories of the future? The two will be tested to their limits. Will the Fae
have their way and is there a future for Duncan and Rachael?

Molly's Laird (Come With Me)

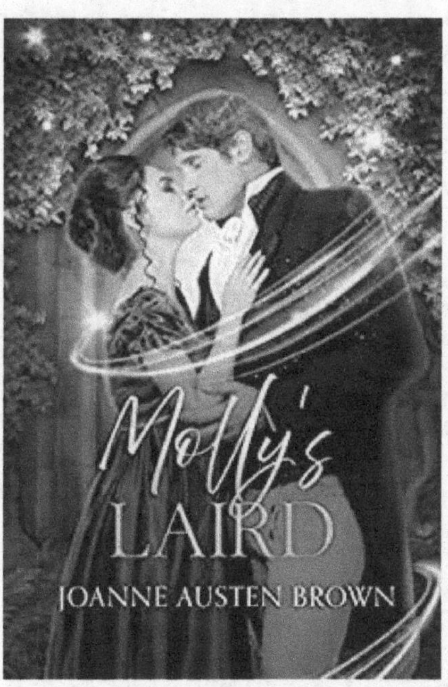

In her own time Molly is a fish out of water. But when she goes back in time to find some peace, after the deaths of all her family, she finds a new beginning.

Can all the promises of the past be true? What about the Fae? And can this handsome man be just for her?

Alasdair misses his brother but understands why he left. He is now Laird but is lonely. Will he find love like Duncan did? Who is the real Molly he cannot stop thinking of? Is she the answer to all he has been searching for? What are the Fae up to?

Always
Delia
JOANNE AUSTEN BROWN

Glenna's
FUTURE
JOANNE AUSTEN BROWN

9 780648 775959